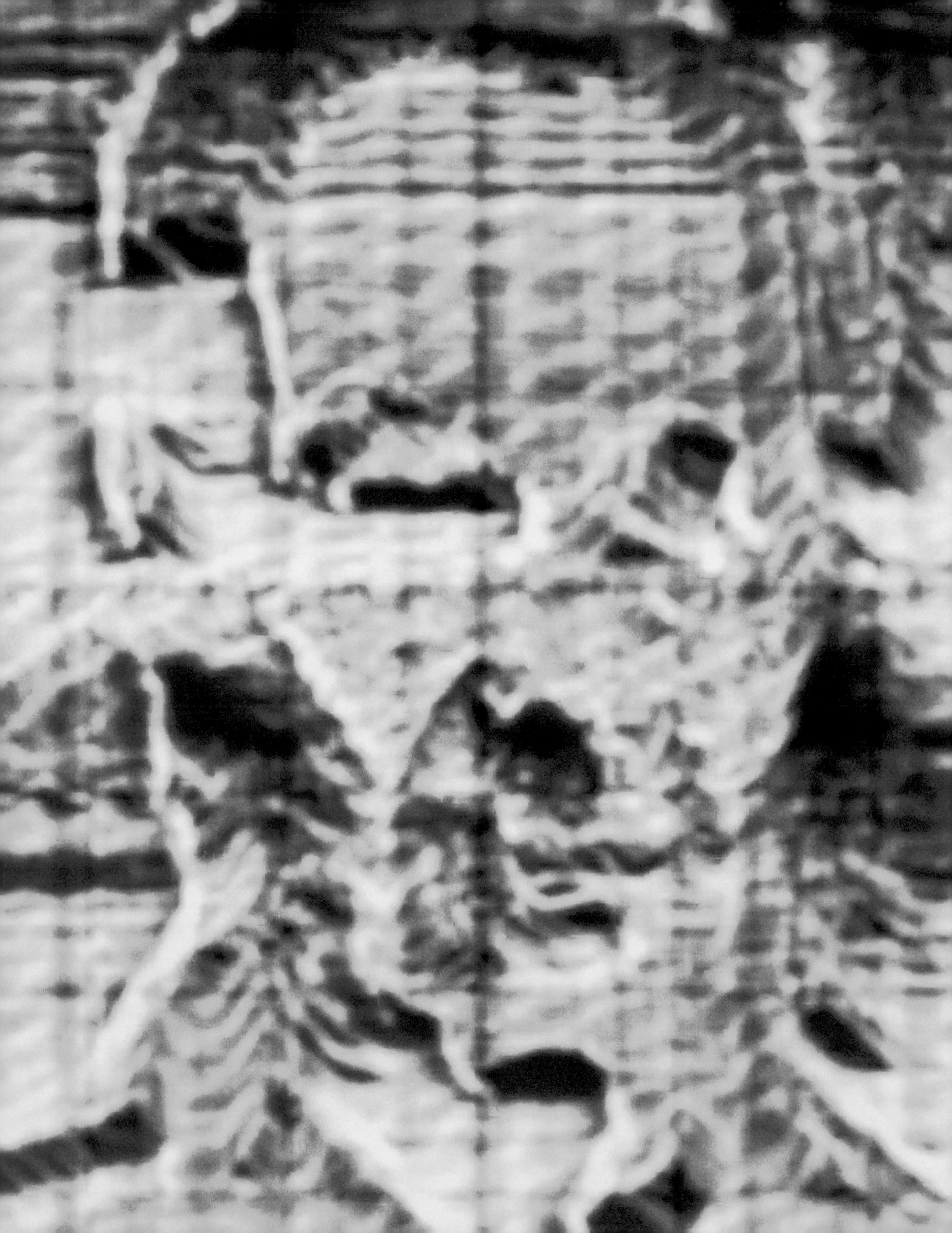

Emma Adler

SIMULATOR [SIC!]NESS

ZF kunststiftung　　modo

do
you
believe
in
truth
???

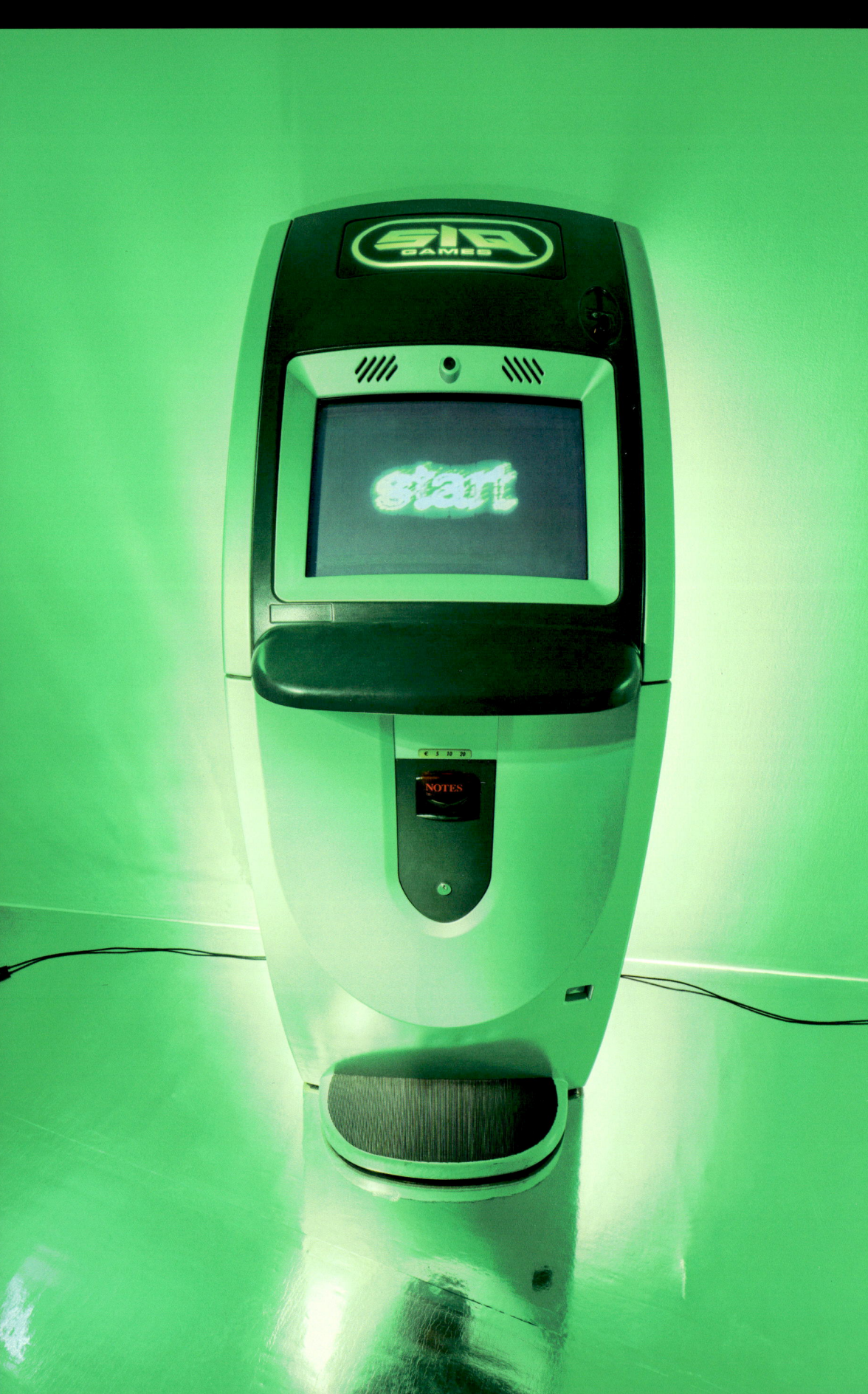

R1-01

R1-01

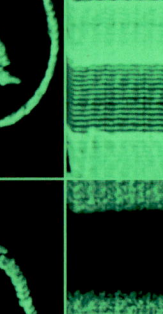

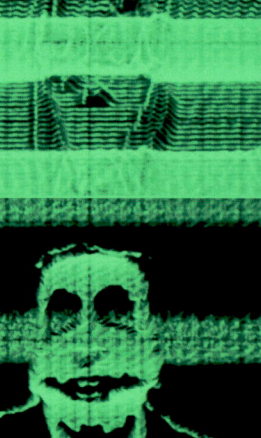

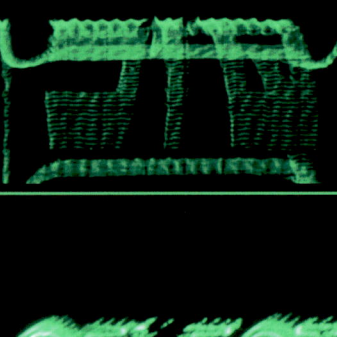

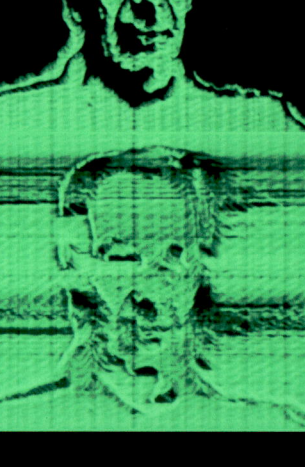

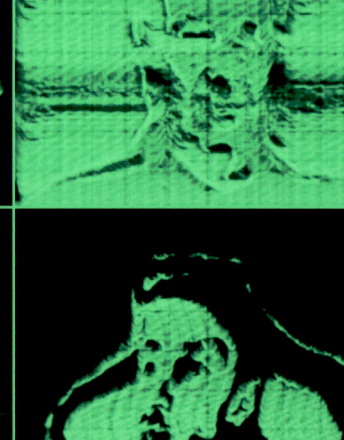

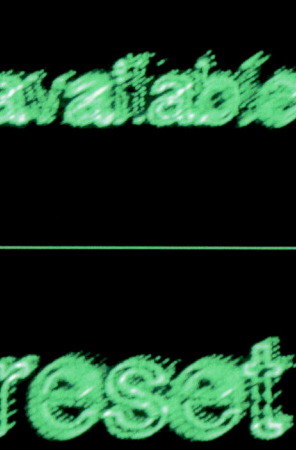

SIQ GAMES

push

no

SELECT content

PLAYER available

reset

R1-02

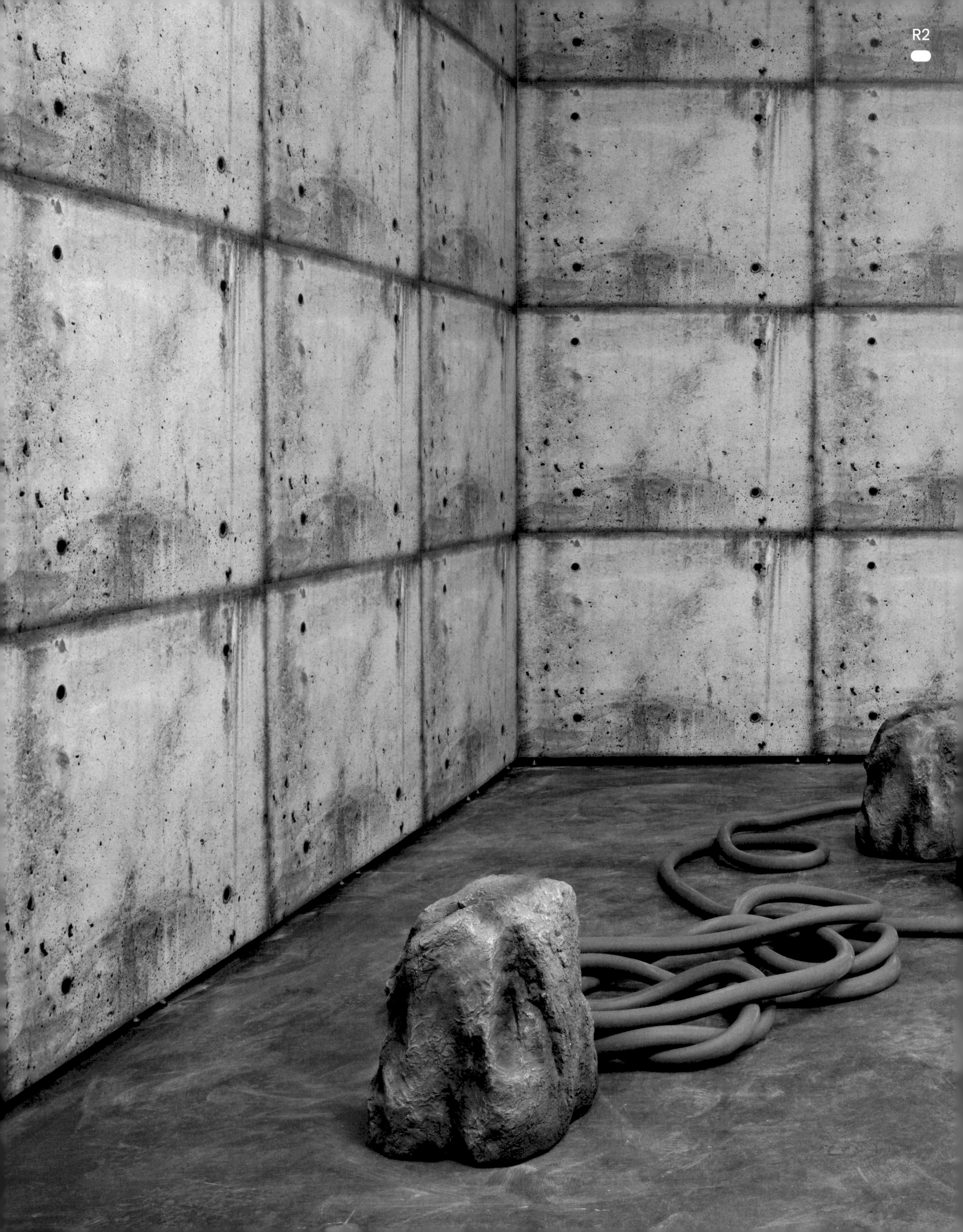

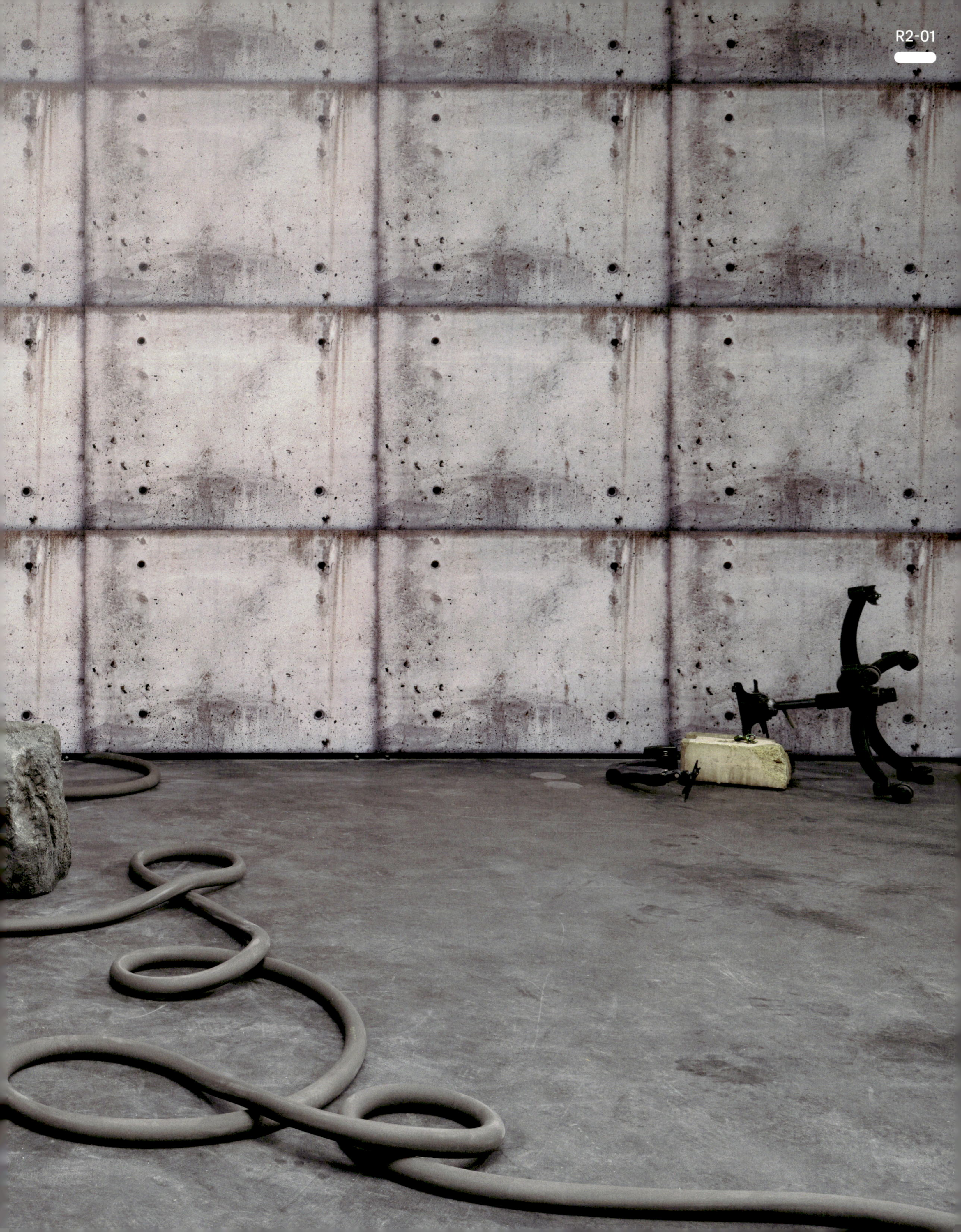

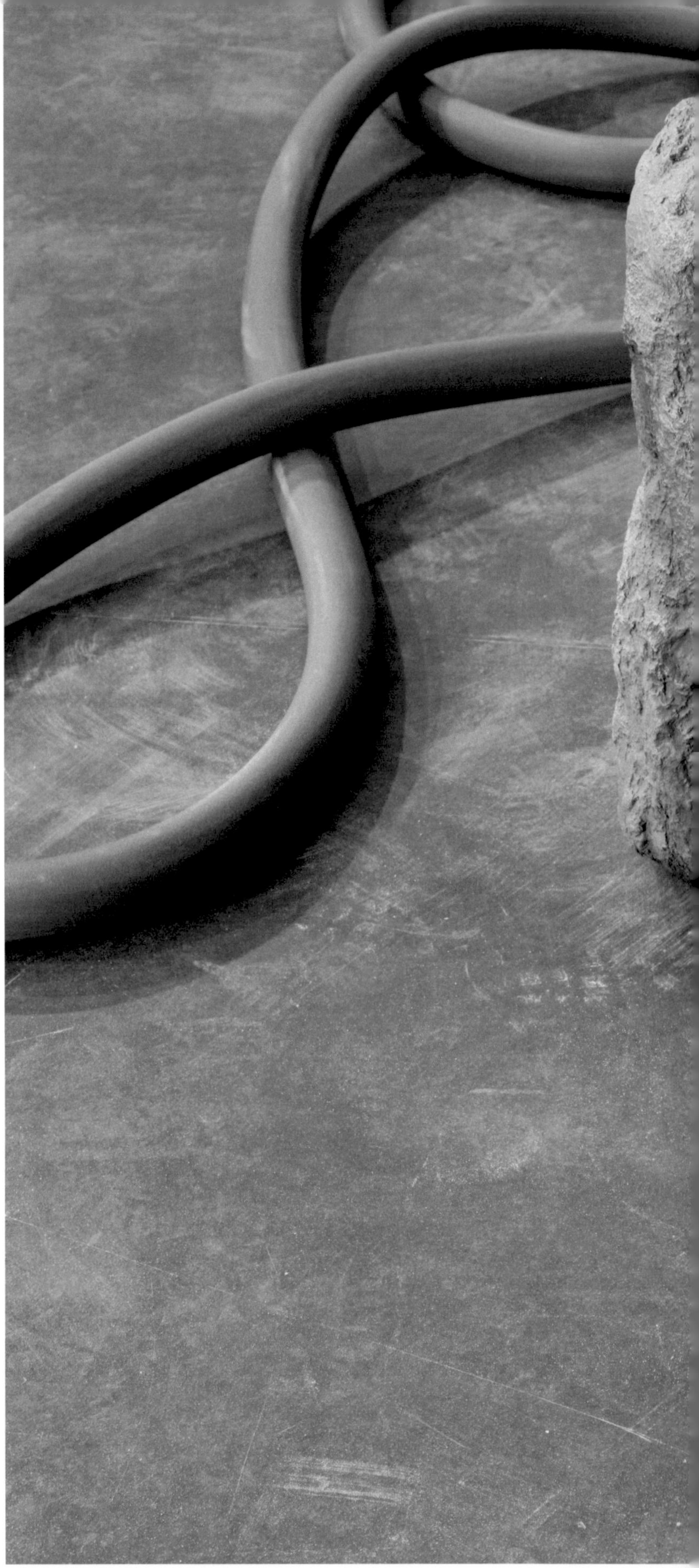

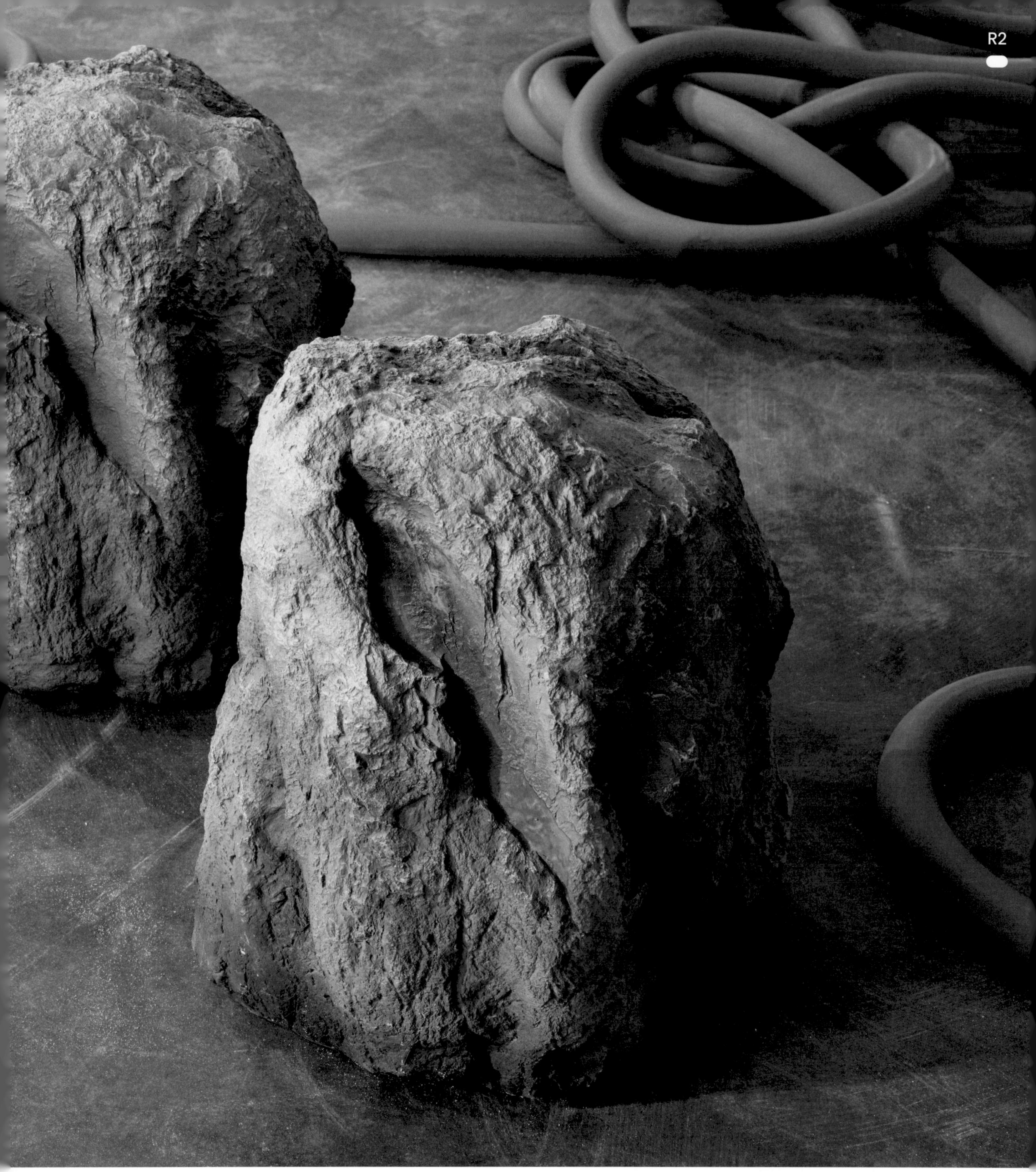

R2-03

R2-04/05

R2-01/02

R2-02

R2-07

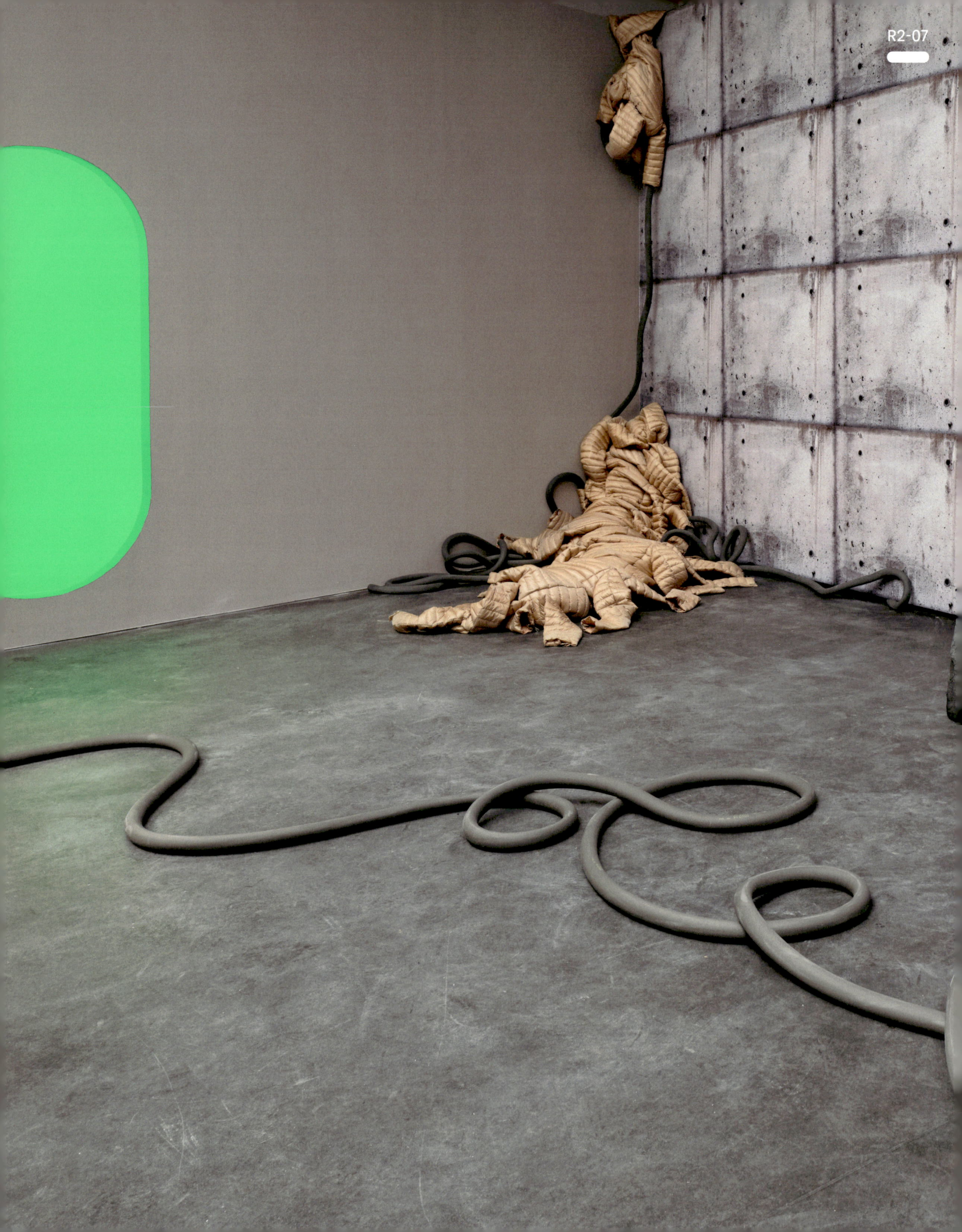

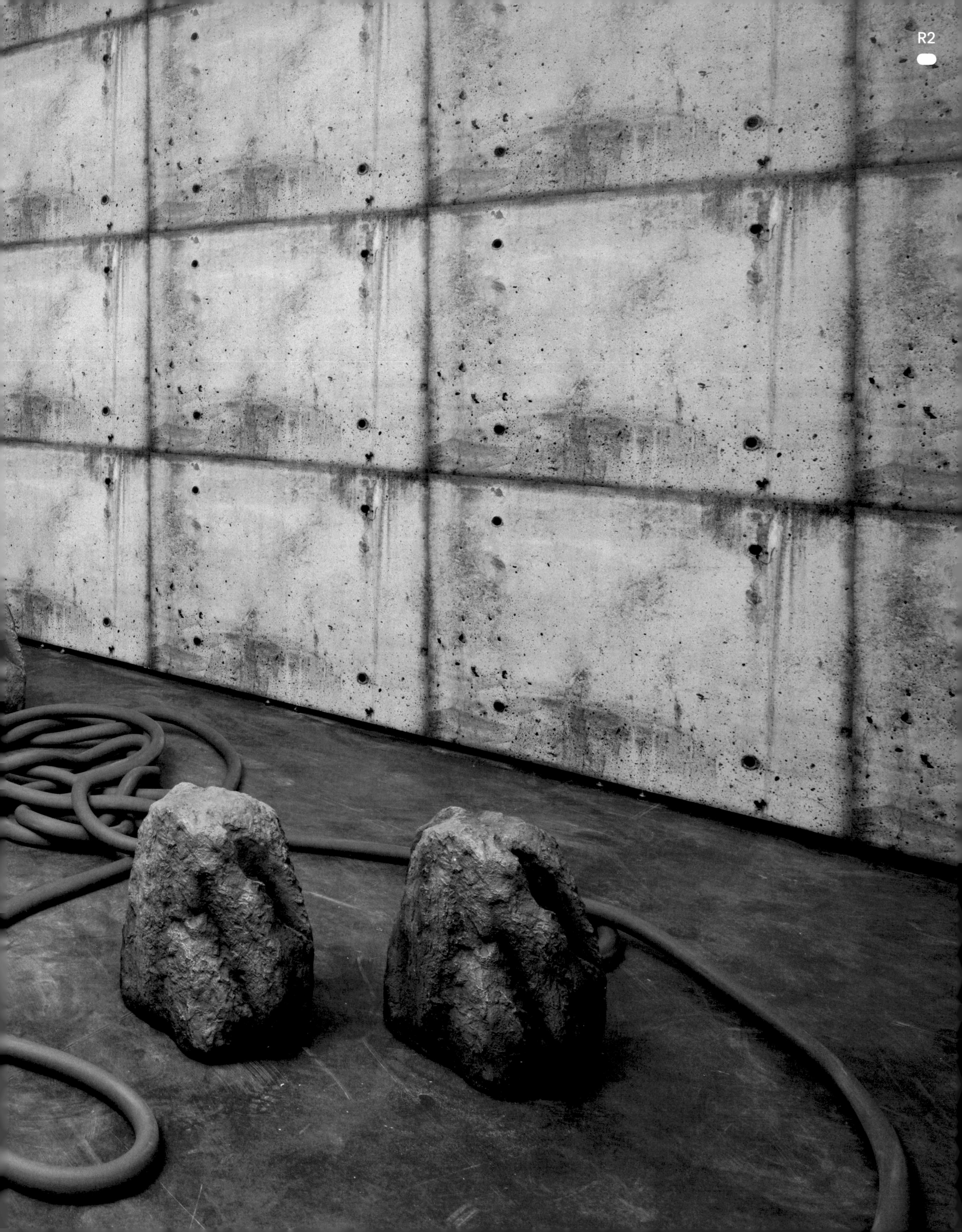

QUERDENKEN

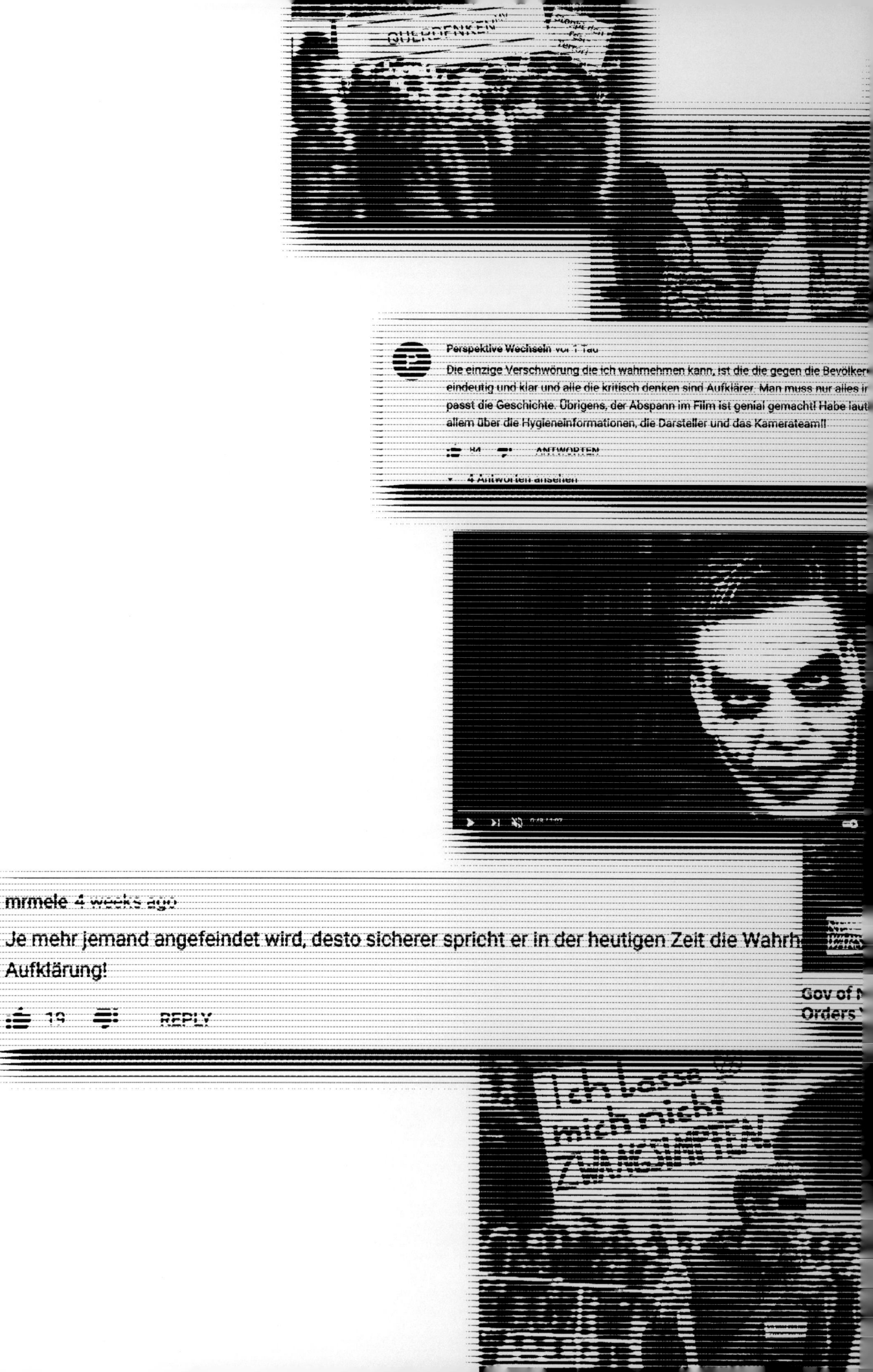

Perspektive Wechseln vor 1 Tag
Die einzige Verschwörung die ich wahrnehmen kann, ist die die gegen die Bevölker
eindeutig und klar und alle die kritisch denken sind Aufklärer. Man muss nur alles in
passt die Geschichte. Übrigens, der Abspann im Film ist genial gemacht! Habe laut
allem über die Hygieneinformationen, die Darsteller und das Kamerateam!!

84   ANTWORTEN

▼ 4 Antworten ansehen

mrmele 4 weeks ago
Je mehr jemand angefeindet wird, desto sicherer spricht er in der heutigen Zeit die Wahrh
Aufklärung!

19   REPLY

Ich lasse mich nicht ZWANGSIMPFEN

Die Realität im Zeitalter ihrer technischen Reproduzierbarkeit

Melina Mercer

Reality in the Age of Technical Reproducibility

Melina Mercer

1. In the beginning there was reality… The search for and finding of new artistic positions traditionally takes place in exhibition contexts, for example in galleries, at fairs, in studios or at biennales. I first came across Emma Adler's art as an installation view of approximately credit card size on a computer screen. Nevertheless the brief impression was enough to trigger an excessive internet research. My interest was therefore not aroused from the original, the artwork itself, but from a duplicate media representation, namely the photo of an exhibition that I was looking at on a screen. This story offers a wonderful entry into Adler's œuvre when she outlines the meta-theme of her artistic analysis: the complex relationships between different levels of reality that have become ever more entangled through the digitalization and technization of our everyday world.

1. Am Anfang war die Realität… Das Suchen und Finden neuer künstlerischer Positionen passiert klassischerweise in Ausstellungskontexten, beispielsweise in Galerien, auf Messen, in Ateliers oder auf Biennalen. Emma Adlers Kunst begegnete mir zum ersten Mal als ungefähr kreditkartengroße Installationsansicht auf einem Computerbildschirm. Trotzdem reichte der kurze Eindruck aus, um eine exzessive Internetrecherche zu triggern. Mein Interesse wurde also nicht von dem Original, dem Kunstwerk selbst geweckt, sondern von einer doppelten medialen Repräsentation, nämlich dem Foto einer Ausstellung, das ich auf einem Bildschirm betrachtete. Diese Geschichte bietet einen wunderbaren Einstieg in Adlers Œuvre, da sie das Metathema ihrer künstlerischen Auseinandersetzungen umreißt: Die komplexen Beziehungen verschiedener Realitätsebenen, die durch die Digitalisierung und Technisierung unserer Alltagswelt immer verwobener werden.

The Internet offers many useful opportunities, yet as a research instrument it has become indispensable in our daily life. From almost anywhere we can immediately search for information, communicate worldwide and receive news in real time. On account of these characteristics many hopes in the new technology have been pinned on the popularisation of the World Wide Web. Exactly as was the case with television, the inventors of the Internet were convinced that with this medium a tool had at last been found to make education accessible to the broad masses. The dream of enlightenment that might liberate each and everyone from their self-imposed immaturity seemed to be within reach. Although the belief in progress of the modern has been extensively deconstructed by postmodern criticism, this hope placed in technology is particularly persistent. This was also so at the beginning of the 2000s. In an issue of *Yahoo! Internet Life* magazine that appeared in December 1999 it was said that through the constant verifiability of claims the Internet would help to oblige politicians to honesty. Tim Berners-Lee, who is regarded as the founder of the World Wide Web, even asserted: "I've always viewed the Web as a tool for democracy and peace."[1] These unreservedly positive evaluations of the World Wide Web and their associated prophesies have not been fulfilled. Despite the sheer endless abundance of available information, data and facts, the Internet has definitely not contributed to an enlightenment, but rather reinforced the post-factual tendencies of perceived truths that were always present. The pluralisation of world views and opinions, and the algorithms of the social media reinforce one's own thinking with their constant affirmation, while at the same time suggesting this would be shared by many others. The result is as many different versions of the truth as there are people who are seeking it.

1 Arends, Timothy: *Predicting the Internet. How Wrong Were They?*, in: TurboFuture, 7 January 2021, under: https://turbofuture.com/internet/Predicting-The-Internet-How-Wrong-Were-They (accessed on 16 October 2021).

2. SIMULATOR [SIC!]NESS Emma Adler's œuvre brings out this ▬▬▬▬▬▬▬ sore point of our time. The exhibition *SIMULATOR [SIC!]NESS* is about conspiracy theories and their dissemination in the Internet. 'Simulator Sickness' describes a feeling of unease that may arise in flight simulators or during a long period in virtual

realities when the perception of the eyes and that of the organs in the ear responsible for balance are in conflict.[2] The writing style borrows the [sic!] that is used in citations as an editorial reference to a mistake or an erroneous piece of information in the original text. In computer languages it may be used within a comment that is, however, only visible to readers of the source code. So already from the title there arises a complex web of references alluding to different forms of deception, fallacy and illusion. At the same time our perception stands in the center of the conflict as the basis for knowledge.

[2] Hänssler, Boris: „*Simulatorkrankheit*". *Seekrank in der virtuellen Realität*, in: Süddeutsche Zeitung, 29 November 2015, under: https://www.sueddeutsche.de/gesundheit/sinne-seekrank-in-der-virtuellen-realitaet-1.2757090. (accessed on 16 October 2021)

On entering the exhibition space, the first thing visitors come upon is a grey machine whose invented brand name *SIQ Games* refers to the title of the exhibition. The arcade game seems to summon us retro-futuristically to choose one of four players. Four counterfeits appear as green flickering outlines that may be identified — or not, depending on how well one is versed in the world of conspiracy theorists. For example, one of the players is Alex Jones, who operates the radical right-wing internet portal *Infowars*. Another one is Ken Jebsen, who with his broadcasting station *Ken FM* disseminates crude conspiracy theories, mostly in the German speaking area. But Adler does not continue to concern herself in the whole exhibition with the narratives that these people disseminate, nor does she try to counter them in some way, even at the end. She does not present us with any further supposedly 'correct' world view, but analyses and deconstructs our present by means of art: four portraits of players from the conspiracy scene are translated into green flickering outlines by means of a machine that is actually used for calibrating films. The reduced faces thus become not only just that, but also resemble the figure of the joker that some of the players up for selection have publicly taken for themselves. Adler creates with her machine a sort of archetype of Internet rogue. At the same time the four men are deprived of their symbols and habitus with which they would otherwise try to convince their audience. Instead of being spellbound by them, the reduction builds up a distance that allows for critical consideration. Although the gaming machine was the first of its type with a touchscreen, trying all the buttons to select a player is to no avail — a further disappointment that offers a reason to examine one's own assumptions and perceptions.

Impfstoffe Graphen-Oxid-tikel für 5G Mind Control?

Spanische Forscher sagen, dass Graphenoxid-Nanopartikel, die in Covid-Impfstoffen gefunden worden, mit Neuronen und anderen Gehirnzellen kompatibel sind. Nanoröhrchen

noch Beschei
sind und wo v
fragen um Erlaubnis. Manchmal hab
ich das Gefühl es hakt ganz gewaltig
in der Birne Leute..

Zeigt mal bisschen C

...desto sicherer spricht er in der heutigen Zeit die Wahrheit. Vielen Dank für die dringend notwendige

Announces New Covid Religion, Says God
Take Experimental Shot

Es hört sich alles verrückt an aber genau
das ist ihr Vorteil! Niemand
nach 75 Jahren Frieden in
eine Clique zu sowas fähig
sind es! Sie haben erst eure
und dann eure Rechte abgeschlachtet...
was bleibt übrig? Sie werden jetzt euch

Heini Klausen vor 1 Tagen
Naja antisemitisch war das jetzt ja irgendwie nicht. Er mag
Christen oder Buddhisten seien können.

ANTWORTEN

Riccarda Ingeborg Schäfer 4 weeks ago
Es bleibt zu wünschen dass alle menschen wach werden und der Realität ins Auge sehen. Jürgen mach weiter.

Forwarded from ATTILA HILDMANN OFFICIAL

Also ich bin eher dafür alle verantwortlichen an den Haaren auf die Straße zu zerren und ins gemächt zu treten bis sie dran verrecken.

▽ Das dritte Kind ist an Sauerstoff-Unterversorgung durch Masken gestorben! Bitte wacht doch endlich auf! Jede x-te Oma die an Altersschwäche stirbt wird uns als Koronatoter verkauft aber bei den Kindern schauen die Medien weg! Masken führen zu Sauerstoffmangel und das führt bei längerer Zeit zu Gehirnschäden! Das bestätigen Neurologen! Die Masken schützen nicht vor Viren, das steht sogar auf der Verpackung! Es ist ein Zeichen des Gehorsams zu Merkel!

Andreas
Frage in dieser Runde
wirklich das man mi
und liebe was erreic
wer hat denn angefa
kacke zu verbreiten
zu verordnen danke

Mind Control: Scientists Engineer 'Magneto' Protein Capable Of Remotely Controlling Brain Behavior

Meinung bilden:

Ich glaube tatsächlich, dass gew
Sehe ich genau SO!!! Zb in osteuropa
sind die menschen knallhart und
zusammen
die ganzen
ch mich
o oft
geht es "gu

SO STIRBST DU
AN DER COVID IMPFUNG

On entering the large exhibition space one is hit by a dystopian scenario: a construction site fence, around which a quilted material trails, is set up crosswise; in the corner a hose of the same material pants frenziedly, and lying on a heap of sand is a green-violet iridescent painted chair. It is reminiscent of a racing car seat, but also of a gaming chair used by online computer gamers and a YouTube content producer called Oli, who Adler came across during her research into the current conspiracy scene. He is another player, who features in the SIQ game mentioned above. The chair appears unreal, strange, to which neither the origin or function can be clearly ascribed. This impression arises because it is the imitation of a chair made of PU foam that has been reduced in form and alienated by the other materiality. The symbols of the manufacturer have also been removed, as have the details of the processing. It looks like a casting. Jean Baudrillard diagnosed in his simulation theory a societal condition in which the symbols are increasingly detached from what they are symbolizing, thereby becoming 'referenceless'.[3] Consumer goods then no longer exist primarily as objects of need, but are consumed in their ideal dimension as a symbol of a particular lifestyle. If the gamers are demonstrating by means of the chair that they are engaging in high performance sport exactly like professional racing drivers, then Web video producers and conspiracy influencers are using it as a symbol of their zeal. As they are sitting the whole day in front of the PC for their audience, researching, commenting and cutting videos, such a comfortable seat is needed. It belongs to the equipment of a hypermasculine Internet warrior. Through the reduction and decontextualization of this consumer good its ideal function becomes visible. From her research journey through the Internet Adler has brought along even more set pieces. The model of a middle ear cochlea sparkles on a site fence foot that is coated with the same flip flop paint as the chair. This organ of the sense of balance refers not only to the title of the exhibition, but is also the symbol of the last player of the quartet: Bodo Schiffmann. He is the face of the 'Querdenker' (Lateral Thinker) movement in Germany, and as a doctor specializes in the phenomenon of vertigo ('Schwindel' in German, with the alternative sense of 'swindle', 'hoax'). To disseminate his views he started off by making use of the channel of his medical practice — which ironically is called 'Schwindelambulanz' (Vertigo Outpatients Clinic).

[3] Baudrillard, Jean: *Simulacra and Simulation,* University of Michigan Press, Ann Arbor MI 1995.

Beim Betreten des großen Raums der Ausstellung trifft man auf ein dystopisches Szenario: Ein Bauzaun, um den sich ein gesteppter Stoff rankt, steht quer; in der Ecke hechelt hektisch ein Schlauch des gleichen Stoffes und auf einem Sandhaufen liegt ein lackierter grünviolett-changierender Stuhl. Er erinnert an einen Rennfahrersitz, aber auch an einen Gaming-Chair, der von Online-Computer-Spieler:innen und einem Youtube-Content-Produzenten namens Oli, auf den Adler bei ihrer Recherche zur aktuellen Verschwörungsszene stieß, benutzt wird. Er ist ein weiterer Spieler, der im oben beschriebenen SIQ Game auftaucht. Der Stuhl erscheint unwirklich, seltsam, lässt sich weder in seiner Herkunft noch in seiner Funktion eindeutig zuordnen. Dieser Eindruck entsteht, weil er die Nachbildung eines Stuhles aus PU-Schaum ist, der in seiner Form reduziert und durch die andere Materialität verfremdet wurde. Die Zeichen der Herstellerfirma wurden genauso entfernt wie Details der Verarbeitung. Er sieht aus wie gegossen. Jean Baudrillard diagnostizierte in seiner Simulationstheorie einen gesellschaftlichen Zustand, in dem sich die Zeichen zunehmend von ihrem Bezeichneten gelöst haben werden und so „referenzlos" geworden sind.[3] Konsumgüter existieren dann nicht mehr primär als Gegenstände des Gebrauchs, sondern werden in ihrer ideellen Dimension als Zeichen für einen bestimmten Lebensstil konsumiert. Demonstrierten die Gamer noch mittels des Stuhls, dass sie genauso wie Profi-Rennfahrer Hochleistungssport betreiben, nutzen ihn Webvideoproduzenten und Verschwörungs-Influencer als Zeichen ihres Fleißes. Da sie für ihr Publikum den ganzen Tag vor dem PC sitzen, recherchieren, kommentieren und Videos schneiden, ist ein solch bequemer Thron vonnöten. Er gehört zur Rüstung eines hypermännlichen Internet-Warriors. Durch die Reduktion und Dekontextualisierung dieses Konsumguts macht sie seine ideelle Funktion sichtbar. Von ihrer Recherchereise durchs Internet hat Adler noch mehr Versatzstücke mitgebracht. Auf einem Bauzaunfuß funkelt das Modell einer Mittelohrschnecke, das mit dem gleichen Flip-Flop-Lack überzogen ist wie der Stuhl. Dieses Organ des Gleichgewichtssinns bezieht sich nicht nur auf den Ausstellungstitel, sondern ist das Symbol des letzten Spielers des Quartetts: Bodo Schiffmann. Er ist das Gesicht der Querdenken-Bewegung in Deutschland und als Arzt auf das Phänomen des Schwindels spezialisiert. Zur Verbreitung seiner Ansichten nutzte er zu Anfang den Kanal seiner medizinischen Praxis, die sich ironischerweise Schwindelambulanz nennt.

[3] Baudrillard, Jean: *Simulacra and Simulation,* University of Michigan Press, Ann Arbor MI 1995.

Der große Ausstellungsraum ist auf zwei Seiten von einer Betonwand eingeschlossen. Bei genauer Betrachtung fällt auf, dass alle Betonfelder exakt gleich aussehen. Sie sind identische Kopien. Gibt es ein Original? Auf einer optischen Spurensuche erinnert die Wand an Sichtbeton, den man von Bunkeranlagen oder temporären Architekturen im urbanen Raum kennt. Aber in diesem Umfeld kann nicht jeder Stein gleich aussehen, es sei denn, es ist ein Fehler in der Matrix. Die Erscheinung von Beton als bildliche Reproduktion kennt man wiederum von Küchen in Betonoptik oder von Beton imitierenden PVC-Belägen. Die naheliegendste Referenz der gestapelten, immer gleichen und leicht verfallenen Betonplatten sind Wände in Computerspielen, in denen Programme mittels digitaler Stempel im Nu ein ganzes Gebäude hochziehen. Wäre dann der programmierte Beton, der ja selbst eine Kopie von Sichtbeton ist, das Original? Und ist das Original die fertige Visualisierung des Betons oder sind es die Zahlen des programmierten Stempels? Schon in seinem 1935 erschienenen Aufsatz *Das Kunstwerk im Zeitalter seiner technischen Reproduzierbarkeit* arbeitete sich Walter Benjamin an der problematischen Dialektik von Original und Kopie, Aura und Zerstörung, Dauer und Flüchtigkeit ab. Er kommt zu dem Schluss, dass schon bei einer Fotografie Bestimmungsversuche zwecklos sind. Ein analoges Foto hat schließlich ein Negativ, das nicht das fertige Produkt ist, aber von dem endlos viele Abzüge gemacht werden können. Angewendet auf unsere Gegenwart, lässt sich der Verlust des originalen Kunstwerks mit dem Verlust einer originären Realität gleichsetzen. Die digitalen Welten und die analoge Realität sind auf unzähligen Ebenen untrennbar miteinander verwoben, wobei jeder einzelne Mensch in seinem ganz eigenen Gemenge lebt.

The large exhibition space is enclosed on two sides by a concrete wall. On closer examination it is clear that all the concrete panels look exactly alike. They are identical copies. Is there an original? On a visual search the wall resembles exposed concrete that one knows from bunkers or temporary architecture in the urban space. But in this environment not every stone can appear the same, unless there is a fault in the matrix. The appearance of concrete as visual reproduction we again know from kitchens in a concrete look, or from PVC surfaces imitating concrete. The nearest reference to stacked concrete slabs that are always identical and slightly decayed are walls in computer games in which programs erect entire buildings by means of digital stamps in no time. Would the programmed concrete, which is itself a copy of exposed concrete, then be the original? And is the original the finalized visualization of the concrete, or is it the numbers of the programmed stamps? Already in his essay *Das Kunstwerk im Zeitalter seiner technischen Reproduzierbarkeit* published in 1935, Walter Benjamin was working on the problematic dialectic of original and copy, aura and destruction, permanence and fleetingness. He comes to the conclusion that attempts at a resolution are already pointless with a photographic image. After all, an analog photo has a negative that is not the finished product, although any number of prints can be made from it. Applied to our present day, the loss of the original art work may be equated with the loss of an original reality. The digital world and the analogous reality are inseparably interwoven on innumerable levels, with each individual person living in his own quite distinctive confusion.

A particular quality of Adler's works is simply that, quite in keeping with the age, they do not describe a dialectic of original and copy, of analog and digital, of truth and falsehood, but all the (concrete) grey in between. In contrast to the conspiracy theorists she is not concerned with simple answers to complex questions. The contradictions of the present are not leveled in any singular narrative, but exposed — for example by a 'faked' concrete wall that is a reverse translation from a virtual world into the analog exhibition space.

Eine besondere Qualität von Adlers Arbeiten ist eben, dass sie ganz zeitgemäß keine Dialektik von Original und Kopie, von analog und digital, von Wahrheit und Lüge beschreiben, sondern das ganze (Beton-)Grau dazwischen. Im Gegensatz zu den Verschwörungstheoretikern geht es ihr nicht um einfache Antworten auf komplexe Fragen. Die Widersprüche der Gegenwart werden in kein singuläres Narrativ eingeebnet, sondern herausgestellt – beispielsweise durch eine „gefakte" Betonwand, die eine Rückübersetzung aus einer virtuellen Welt in den analogen Ausstellungsraum ist.

3. Ein kritisches Fazit Walter Benjamin stellte für seine Zeit, besonders in Bezug auf den Film, die These auf, dass die Menschen eine neue Wahrnehmung lernen müssten. Das neue Medium gilt es zu lesen und zu verstehen. Wir besitzen heute fast selbstverständlich die mediale Kompetenz Filme zu lesen, doch für die Neuen Medien, das Internet, Augmented und Virtual Reality fehlt sie noch. Adlers Arbeiten verraten uns etwas über unsere Gegenwart. Die Dekonstruktion, Dekontextualisierung, mediale Übersetzung, Verfremdung, Reduktion und die digitalen Kulturtechniken wie das Copy-Paste lehren uns eine neue Wahrnehmung, die es braucht, um mit Benjamin der neuen Geschwindigkeit und Beschleunigung unseres Zeitalters gewachsen zu sein.

Das Verständnis der neuen Technologien in ihren Meta-Sprachen und der Geisteshaltungen, von denen sie durchdrungen sind, bedarf eines aufgeklärten Menschen mit technologischer Bildung. Gerade hier kann die Kunst einen wichtigen Beitrag leisten. Denn auch wenn wir in einer Welt leben, in der Maschinen und Technologien immer umfassender menschliche Arbeit ersetzen, bleibt das kritische Denken weiterhin die Domäne des Menschen.

3. A critical summary Walter Benjamin put forward a thesis for his time, particularly in relation to film, that people ought to learn a new perception. The new medium made it important to read and to understand. Today we possess almost as a matter of course the media competence to read films, yet for the new media, the Internet, augmented and virtual reality it is still lacking. Adler's works tell us something about our present. Deconstruction, decontextualization, media translation, alienation, reduction and the digital culture technologies, like copy-and-paste, teach us a new perception that is required in order to come to terms along with Benjamin with the new speed and acceleration of our age.

Understanding of the new technologies in their meta languages and of the mindsets in which they are steeped, requires an enlightened person with a technology education. It is exactly here that art can make an important contribution. For even if we live in a world in which machines and technology replace human work ever more comprehensively, critical thinking will continue to remain the domain of people.

enkt ihr alle
eden Freude
kann? -
en solche
Maßnahmen
er wir

nicht
n weiter
er
ve und
h nicht
ieg,
t eure
keine
nicht

die die gegen die Bevölkerung gerichtet ist! Die ist
ührer. Man muss nur alles ins Gegenteil setzten dann
n müssen, vor

diese Leute nicht, die hätten ja auch moslems

R2-03

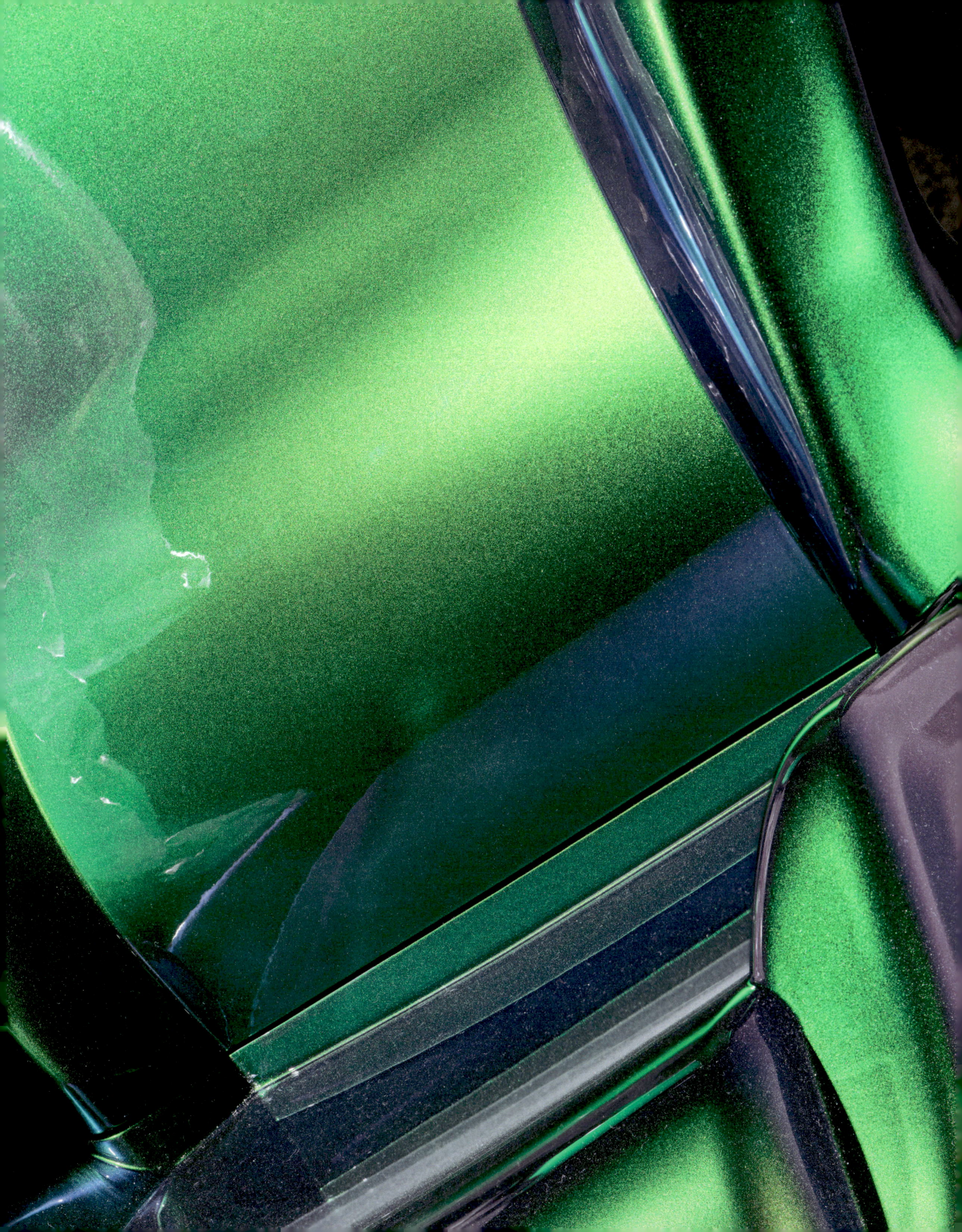

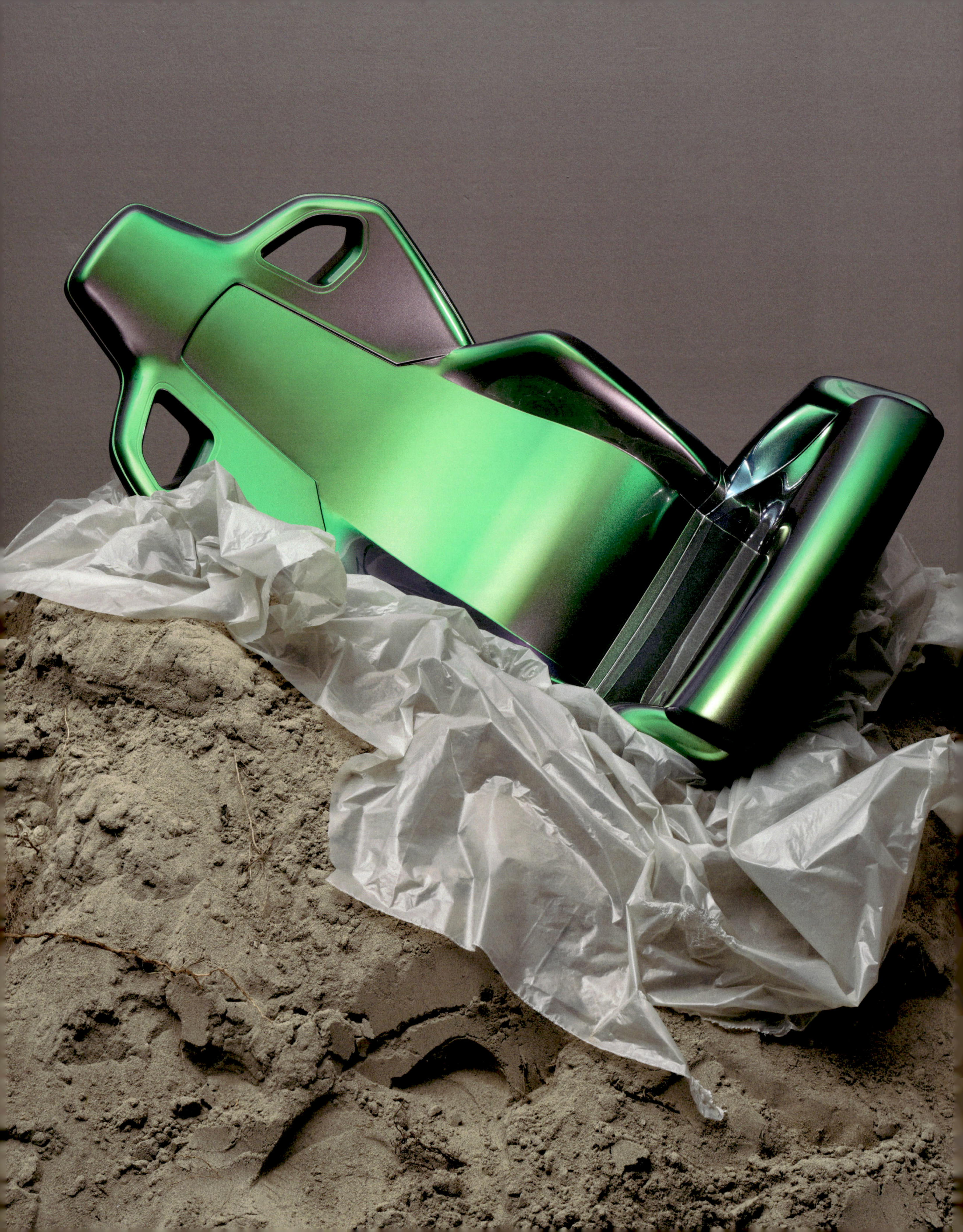

R2-03

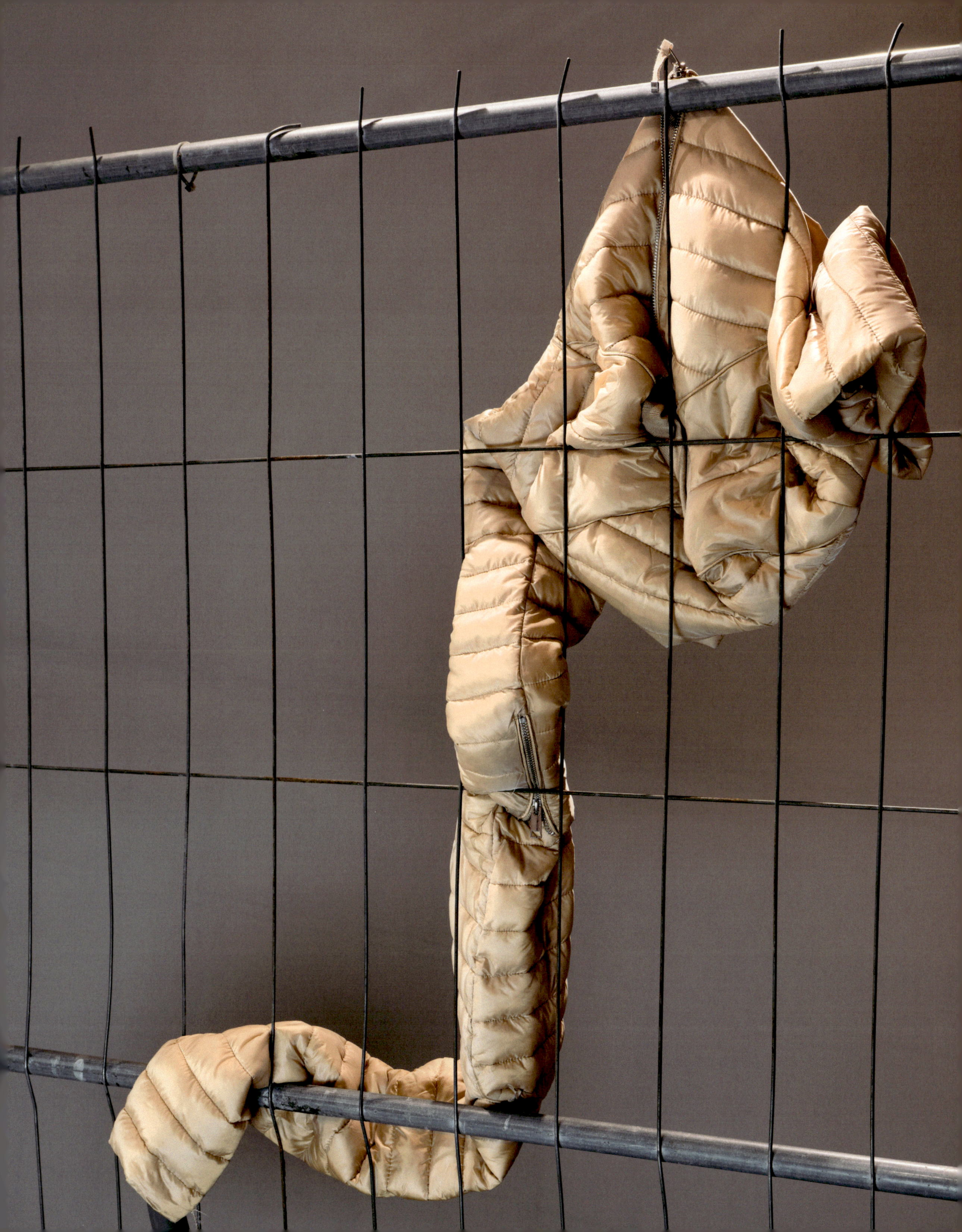

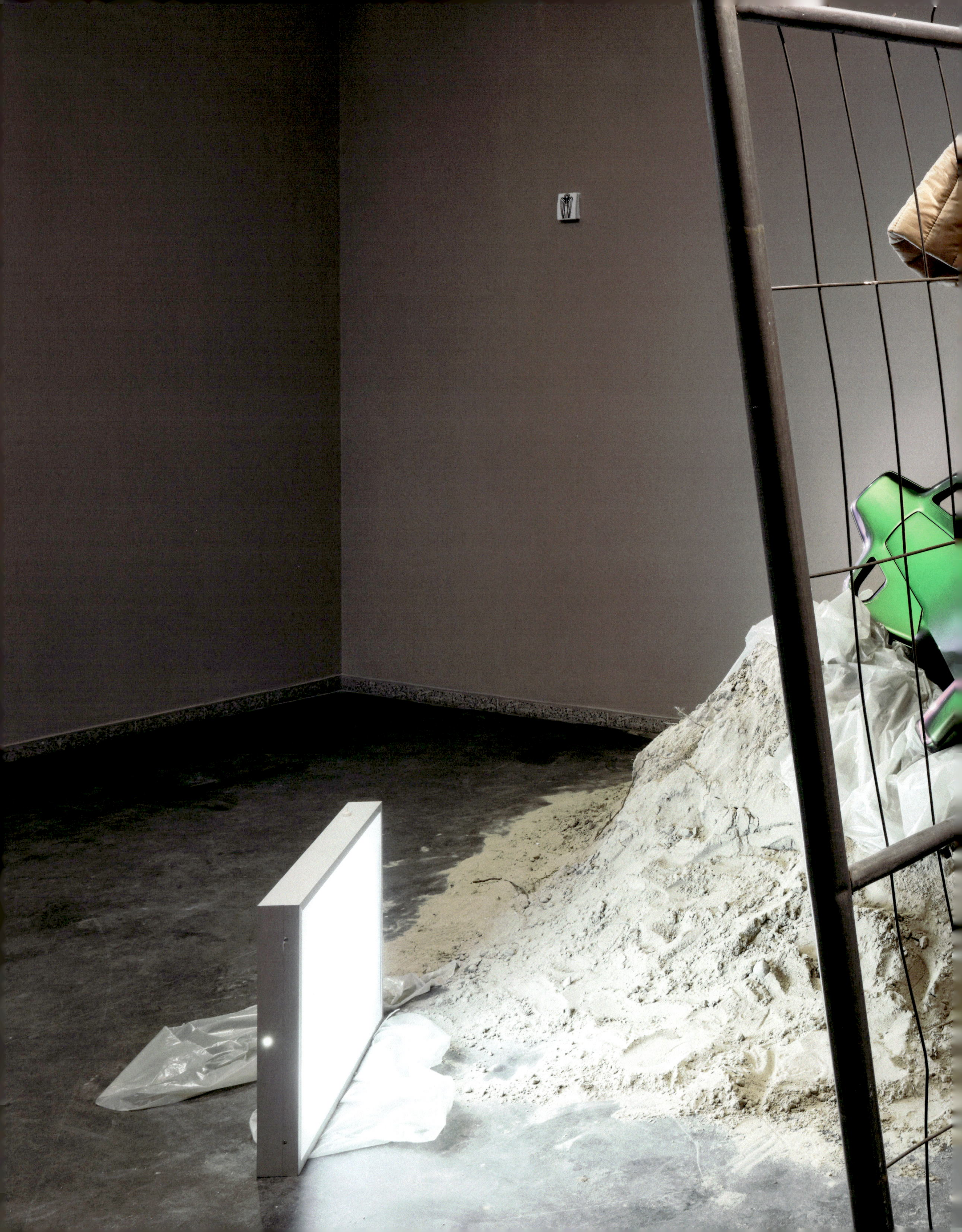

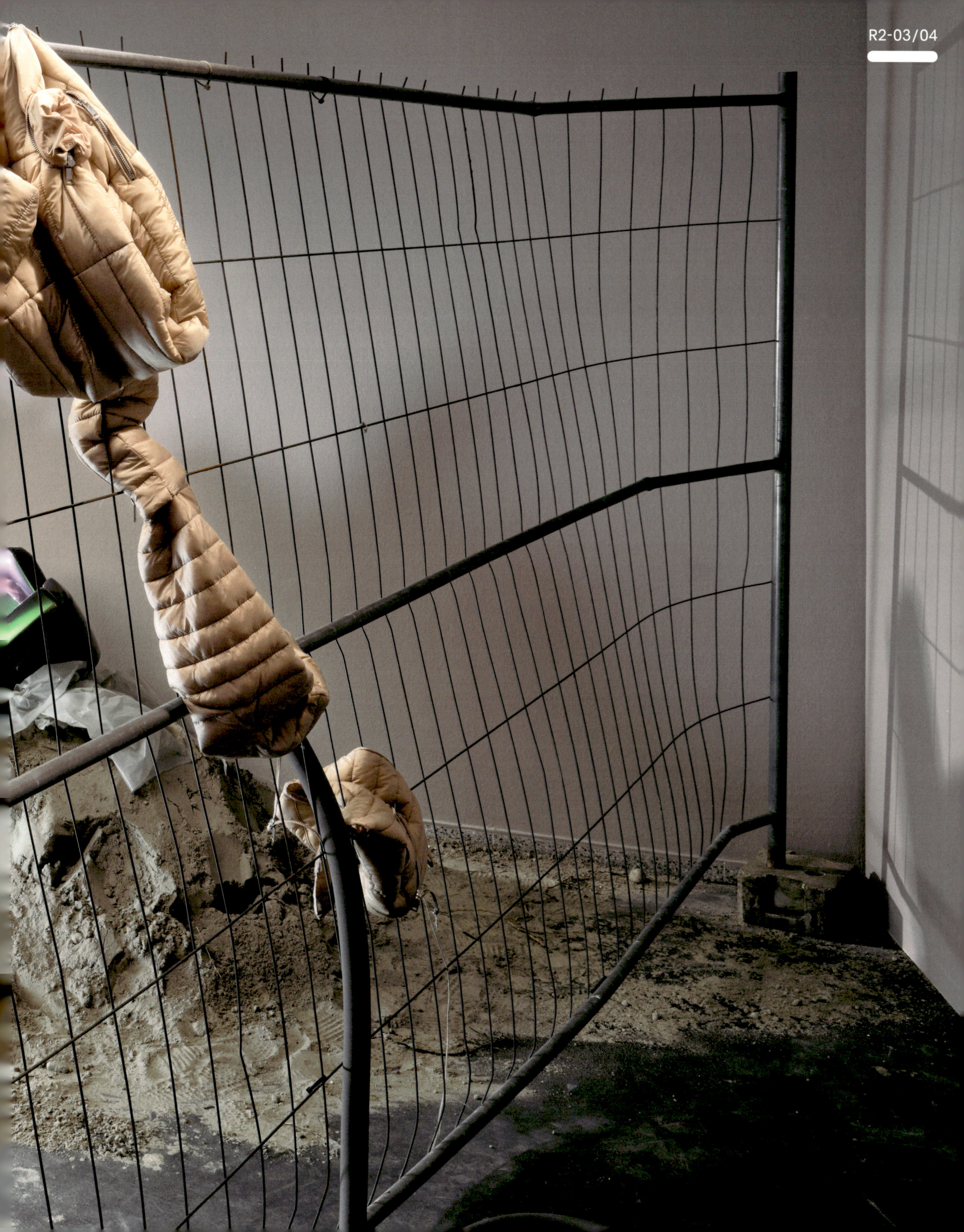

R2-03

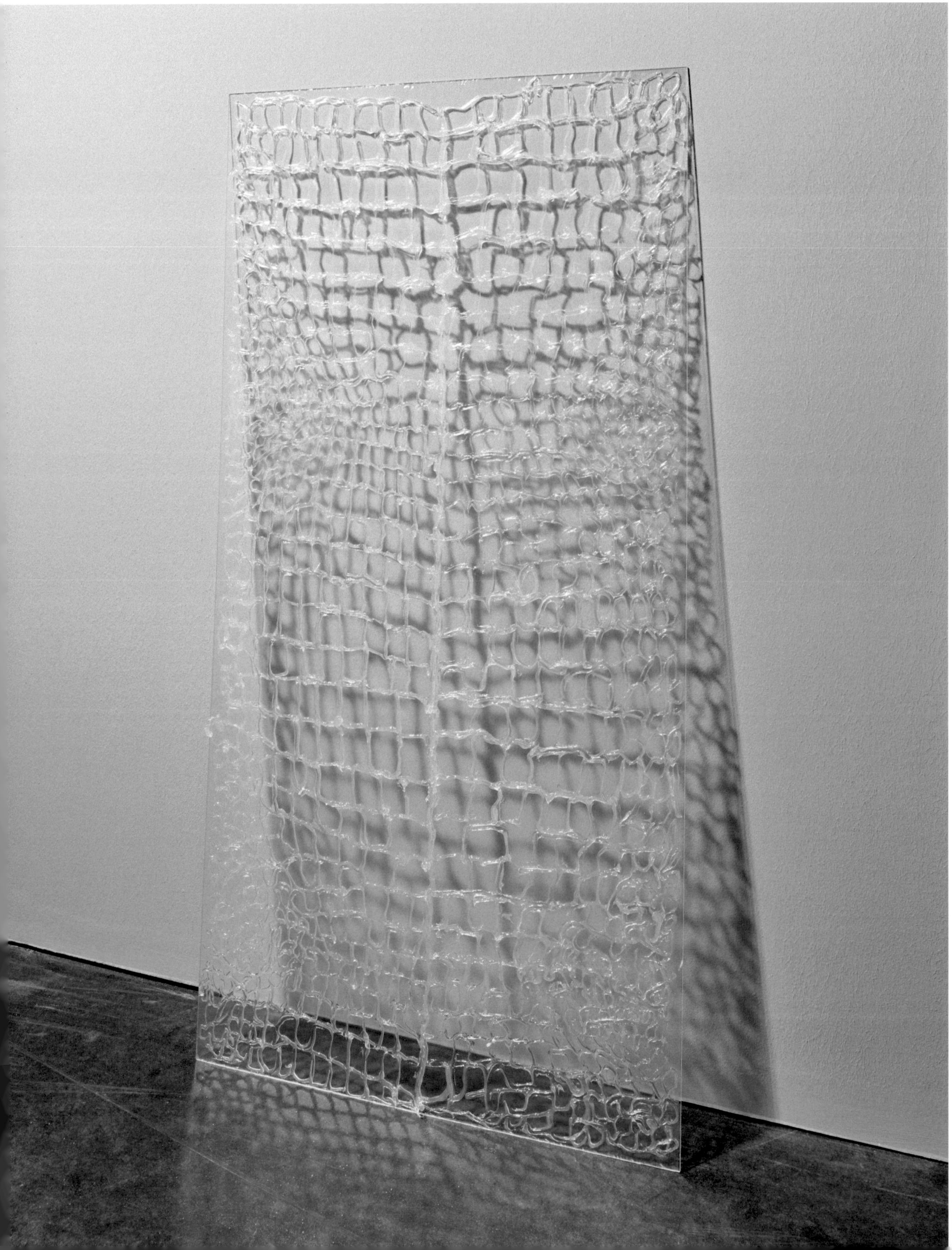

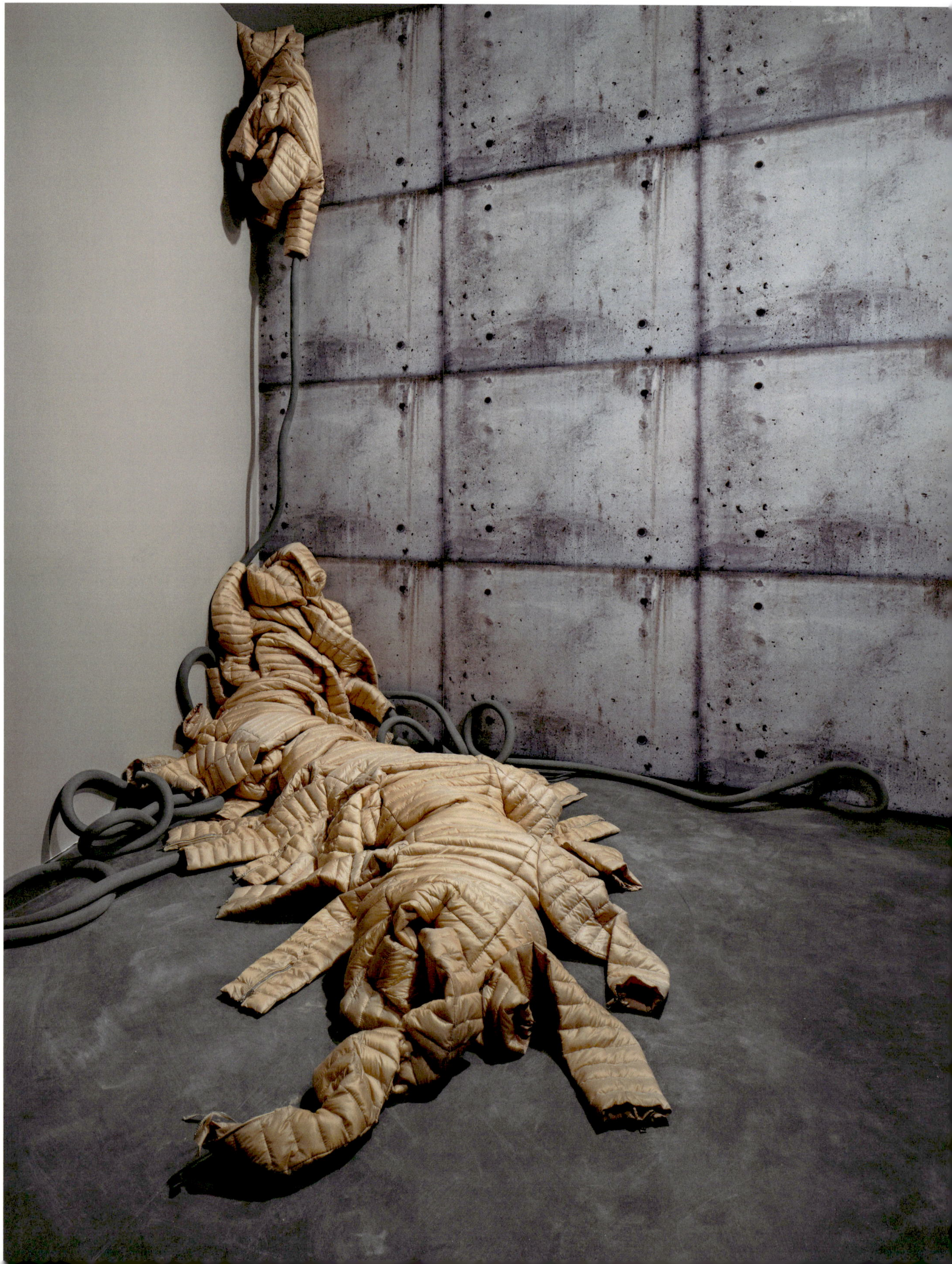

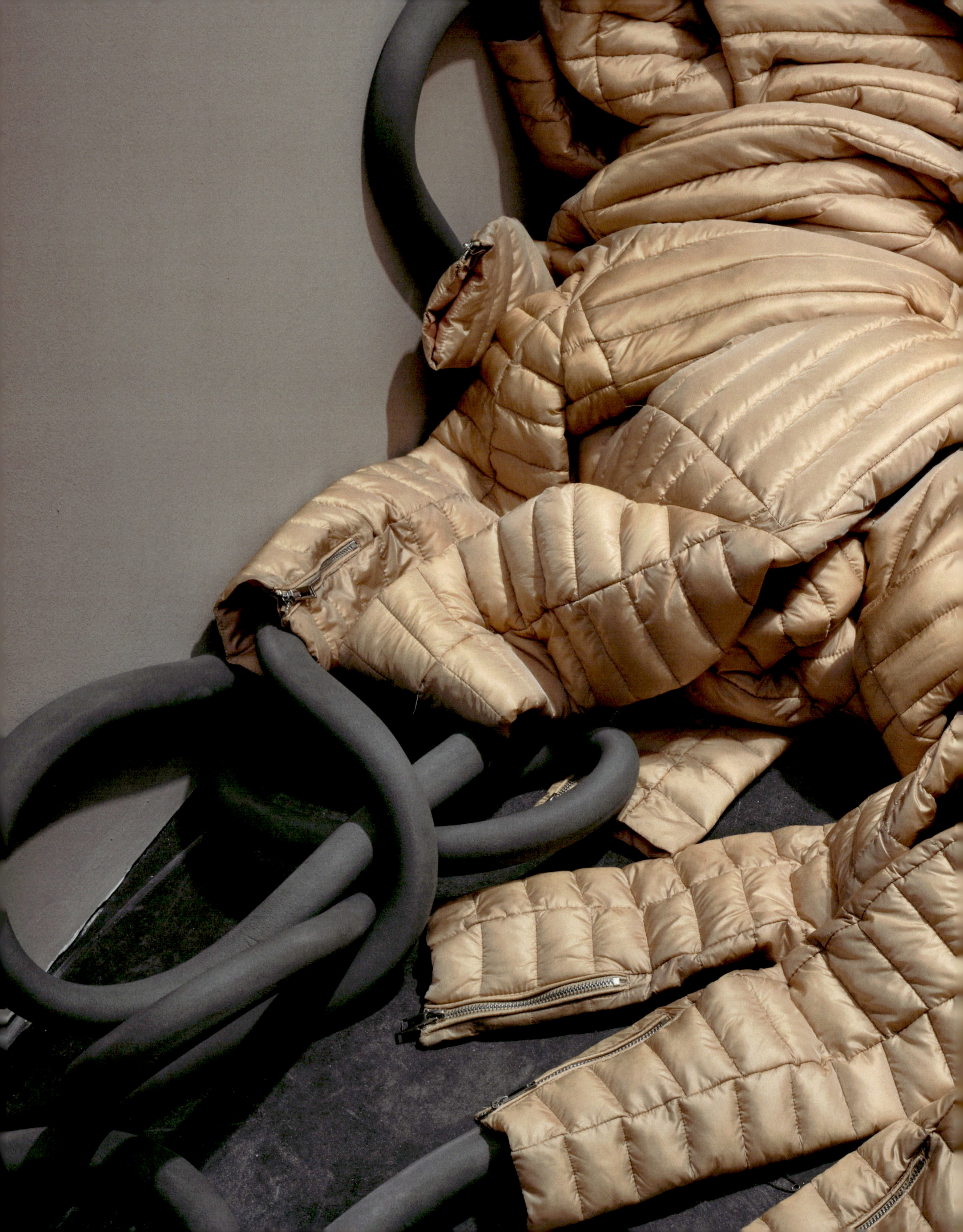

R2-07

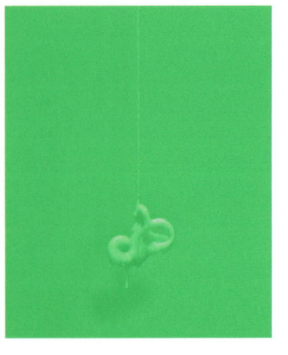

SIMULATOR [SIC!]NESS 2021

R1-02 SIMULATOR [SIC!]NESS (Glitch-I)
3D-Druck einer Mittelohrschnecke, eingefärbtes Silikon, von der Decke hängend
3D printing of a middle ear cochlea, colored silicone, hanging from the ceiling

R2-07 SIMULATOR [SIC!]NESS (Qreatur2)
(2-teilig), Steppjacken, Stoff, Füllmaterial, Motoren, Haken, Schaumstoffschlauch
(2 pieces), quilted jackets, fabric, padding, motors, hooks, foam tube

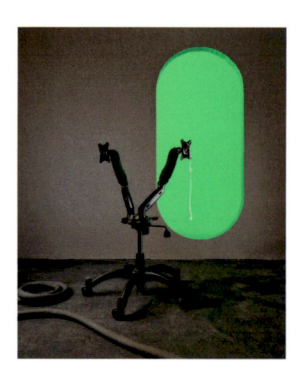

R2-06 SIMULATOR [SIC!]NESS (hybrid1)
Bürostuhl, Monitorarm, Gaffa-Tape, Silikon
Office chair base, monitor arm, gaffer tape, silicone

R2-05 SIMULATOR [SIC!]NESS (reptiled)
Plexiglas, Silikon
Plexiglass, silicone

REALM1 (corridor)
Holz, Rigips, Farbe, Spiegelfolie
Wood, plasterboard, paint, mirror foil

R1-01 SIMULATOR [SIC!]NESS (SIQ Games)
Spielautomat, Lack, Video (01:37 Min, Loop), Sound, Neonröhre, 2 Ringleuchten
Slot machine, varnish, video (01:37 min, loop), sound, neon tube, 2 ring lights

REALM2 (desert of the real)
Tapete: Druck, Maße variabel; Kunststeine: Glasfaser, Farbe; Schaumstoffschlauch, Erde, Sand, Bauzaun, Leuchtkasten mit manipulierten Neonröhren
Wallpaper: print, dimensions variable; artificial stones: fiberglass, paint; foam tube, soil, sand, site fence, light box with manipulated neon tube

R2-01 SIMULATOR [SIC!]NESS
(hybrid2/broken)
Bürostuhl, Monitorarm, Bauzaunfuß, Gaffa-Tape
Office chair base, monitor arms, site fence base, gaffer tape

R2-04 SIMULATOR [SIC!]NESS
(Qreatur1)
Steppjacken, Steppstoff (an Bauzaun), Schaumstoffschlauch
Quilted jackets, quilted fabric (on fence), foam tube

R2-02 SIMULATOR [SIC!]NESS
(sick_object)
3D-Druck einer Mittelohrschnecke, Autoeffektlack
3D printing of a middle ear cochlea, car effect paint

R2-03 SIMULATOR [SIC!]NESS
([sic!] object)
PU-Schaum, Autoeffektlack, Sandhaufen mit 3D-Druck einer Mittelohrschnecke, Acrylfarbe
PU foam, car effect paint, pile of sand with 3D printing of a middle ear cochlea, acrylic paint

R2-06

Biografie / Biography

Emma Adler, geboren in Besch, hat in Saarbrücken und Berlin Freie Kunst studiert. An der Weißensee Kunsthochschule Berlin war sie bis 2015 Meisterschülerin bei Else Gabriel. Ihre Abschlussarbeit *EEEEF#GE* (2015) wurde mehrfach ausgezeichnet und 2017 in der Ausstellung *Rundgang 50Hertz* in Kooperation mit dem Hamburger Bahnhof, Museum für Gegenwart, Berlin, präsentiert.

In ihren Projekten, die um den Themenkomplex Fake kreisen, fordert Adler gewohnte Betrachtungsweisen heraus und hinterfragt vermeintliche Gewissheiten über das Verhältnis von Realität und medialer Repräsentation. Der Schwerpunkt ihrer raumgreifenden multimedialen Installationen liegt seit 2017 auf Verschwörungstheorien und der damit verbundenen Frage nach verschiedenen Realitätsebenen. Die Einzelausstellungen *SUPERFLARE* (2019) und *REΔLITY SHOW* (2018) sind Teil einer Reihe komplexer Installationen, die sich mit dieser Thematik beschäftigen. In ihrer jüngsten Arbeit *SIMULATOR [SIC!]NESS* (2021) beleuchtet Adler Merkmale und Mechanismen konspiratorischer Konzepte im postfaktischen Zeitalter zwischen Pandemie und Populismus. *SIMULATOR [SIC!]NESS* ist der erste Teil einer neuen Werkreihe, die 2022 fortgeführt wird.

Adlers Arbeiten waren in zahlreichen Gruppen- und Einzelausstellungen vertreten, u. a. im Arp Museum Bahnhof Rolandseck, im Neuen Kunstverein Gießen, im Kunsthaus Dahlem, im Kunstverein Bremerhaven, im Zeppelinmuseum Friedrichshafen und im KINDL – Zentrum für zeitgenössische Kunst, Berlin, sowie in Kopenhagen und New York. Dort war sie 2017, gefördert durch das Künstlerhaus Schloss Balmoral, Artist in Residence. 2021 war Emma Adler Stipendiatin der ZF Kunststiftung; vom BBK Bundesverband wurde ihr eine Förderung für Innovative Kunstprojekte zugesprochen. 2022 wird sie im Rahmen des Saarlandstipendiums an der Akademie der Künste in Berlin leben und arbeiten.

Emma Adler, born in Besch, studied liberal art in Saarbrücken and Berlin. At the Weißensee Kunsthochschule Berlin until 2015 she was a master pupil under Else Gabriel. Her final project *EEEEF#GE* (2015) has been honored several times. In 2017 it was presented in the exhibition *Rundgang 50Hertz* in cooperation with the Hamburger Bahnhof, Museum für Gegenwart, Berlin.

In her projects, which revolve around fakeness themes, Adler challenges familiar points of view, questioning supposed certainties about the relationship of reality and media representation. Since 2017 the focus of her expansive multimedia installations has been conspiracy theories and the associated issue of different levels of reality. The solo exhibitions *SUPERFLARE* (2019) and *REΔLITY SHOW* (2018) are part of a series of complex installations concerning this theme. In her latest work *SIMULATOR [SIC!]NESS* (2021) Adler sheds light on the characteristics and mechanisms of conspiracy concepts in the postfactual age between the pandemic and populism. *SIMULATOR [SIC!]NESS* is the first part of a new series of works that is continuing into 2022.

Adler's works have been represented in numerous group and solo exhibitions, including: at the Arp Museum Bahnhof Rolandseck, the Neuer Kunstverein Gießen, the Kunsthaus Dahlem, the Kunstverein Bremerhaven, the Zeppelinmuseum Friedrichshafen and the KINDL — Zentrum für zeitgenössische Kunst, Berlin, as well as in Copenhagen and New York. She was Artist in Residence there in 2017, sponsored by the Künstlerhaus Schloss Balmoral. In 2021 Emma Adler received a scholarship from the ZF Kunststiftung; she was also awarded a sponsorship for innovative art projects from the BBK Bundesverband. In 2022 under the Saarland scholarship she will live and work at the Akademie der Künste in Berlin.

Impressum Edition Notice

Dieser Katalog erscheint anlässlich der Ausstellung *Emma Adler: SIMULATOR [SIC!]NESS* der ZF Kunststiftung im Zeppelin Museum Friedrichshafen vom 26. November 2021 bis 9. Januar 2022.
This catalogue is published on the occasion of the exhibition *Emma Adler: SIMULATOR [SIC!]NESS* held by the ZF Art Foundation at Zeppelin Museum Friedrichshafen, November 26, 2021 until January 9, 2022.

Herausgeber Editor/s: Matthias Lenz, Regina Michel, ZF Kunststiftung, 88038 Friedrichshafen, www.zf-kunststiftung.com
Redaktion Managing Editor/s: HFS Studio
Text Text: Milena Mercer
Übersetzung Translation: Peter Lilley
Lektorat Copy Editing: Katharina Gewehr
Gestaltung Design: HFS Studio, www.hfs-studio.com
Fotonachweis Photo Credits: Rafael Krötz
Gesamtherstellung Printed by:
DZA Druckerei zu Altenburg GmbH
Erschienen bei Published by: modo Verlag, Freiburg i. Br.

Die Deutsche Nationalbibliothek verzeichnet diese Publikation in der Deutschen Nationalbibliografie; detaillierte bibliografische Daten sind im Internet über http://dnb.dnb.de abrufbar.
The Deutsche Nationalbibliothek lists this publication in the Deutsche Nationalbibliografie; detailed bibliographic data are available online at http:/dnb.dnb.de.

Copyright Copyright © 2022
für diese Ausgabe for this edition:
Kunststiftung der ZF Friedrichshafen AG
und and modo Verlag, Freiburg i. Br.
für den Text bei der Autorin
for the text belongs to the author
für die abgebildeten Werke bei der Künstlerin
for the selected works rests with the artist
© VG Bild-Kunst, Bonn 2021, Emma Adler
modo Verlag GmbH, Freiburg i. Br., www.modoverlag.de

Printed in Germany
Auflage Number of copies: 750
ISBN 978-3-86833-310-7

Emma Adler
www.emma-adler.de

Dank an Thanks to:
Ich danke allen, die bei der Realisierung des Projekts beteiligt waren und Stipendium, Ausstellung sowie diese Publikation ermöglicht haben, insbesondere Sven Beckstette, der mich vorschlagen hat, der ZF Kunststiftung (Matthias Lenz, Regina Michel, Talina Palmer) und dem Zeppelin Museum Friedrichshafen (Claudia Emmert, Ina Neddermeyer, Caro Gellermann, Dominik Busch, Caroline Wind, Yannik Scheurer sowie dem Technikteam).
I would like to thank everyone who was involved in the realization of the project and who made the scholarship, exhibition and this publication possible, especially Sven Beckstette, who nominated me to the ZF Art Foundation (Matthias Lenz, Regina Michel, Talina Palmer) and the Zeppelin Museum Friedrichshafen (Claudia Emmert, Ina Neddermeyer, Caro Gellermann, Dominik Busch, Caroline Wind, Yannik Scheurer and the technical team).

Herzlicher Dank an Special thanks to:
Pascal Ignatius Hector (für die Videokollaboration for the video collaboration), Milena Mercer, Laura Helena Wurth, Claudia Emmert (für die Worte und Texte zu meiner Arbeit for words and text about my work), Sebastian Fischer und Pascal Schönegg (Gestaltung Design), Mathias Schwarz, Joni Majer, Caroline Streck, Aneta Kajzer, Natalie Brück, Dagmara Genda, Ada Van Hoorebeke, Anna Posch (für eure Hilfe und Unterstützung for your help and support).

Außerdem gilt mein Dank Also thanks to:
HFM Modell & Formenbau GmbH – Jürgen Fularczyk,
Arnold Stahl- und Fahrzeugbau GmbH,
RECARO Gaming GmbH,
Marko Mandic.

reset
reset
reset